Lucy's
Quiet
Book

Lucy's Quiet Book

Angela Shelf Medearis

Illustrated by
Lisa Campbell Ernst

Green Light Readers
Harcourt, Inc.
Orlando   Austin   New York   San Diego   Toronto   London

Lucy had six brothers. They were all very noisy.
Sometimes they yelled.
Sometimes they cried.
Sometimes they laughed really loud.

Lucy was very quiet.

When Lucy's house got too loud, she went to the library. The library was quiet, and Lucy liked to help Mrs. Stone, the children's librarian. "How is my helper today?" Mrs. Stone always asked. Lucy just smiled.

One day, Mrs. Stone said, "I have a special
book just for you. It's a story about a girl
who has six brothers."
Lucy took the book and read it. She smiled.
Then she took the book home.

Timmy and Tommy were yelling.
Billy and Bobby were crying.
Sid and Sammy were laughing really loud.
The house was very, very, very noisy!

Lucy had an idea.

Suddenly, Timmy, Tommy, Billy, Bobby, Sid, and Sammy were quiet. Lucy could be as loud as they were! Lucy surprised herself most of all. She grinned and began to read.

The next day, Lucy took the book back
to the library. When she got there, she
couldn't believe her ears.

Children were yelling.
Children were crying.
Children were laughing really loud.

Lucy knew just what to do.

Suddenly, the library was quiet.
Lucy grinned and began to read.

"Thank you, Lucy," said Mrs. Stone. "You read that book very well!"

"This is my quiet book," said Lucy. "Everyone gets quiet as soon as I start reading it."

"I wonder why that is," said Mrs. Stone.

Lucy just smiled.

Think About It

1. What makes Lucy's brothers and the children at the library become quiet?

2. How do the author and illustrator show that Lucy changes during the story?

3. What do you like most about the story?

A Helper Award

Lucy was a good helper
at the library.

Make an award for Lucy.

WHAT YOU'LL NEED

paper

crayons or markers

scissors

glue

1 Draw a circle and ribbon, then cut them out.

2 Write something nice about Lucy on the circle.

Lucy is a good helper.

3 Write why Lucy is a good helper.

Lucy read to the other kids.

4 Glue the ribbon to the circle.

Lucy is a good helper.

Lucy read to the other kids.

5 Share your award.
Tell why Lucy is a good helper.

Now make awards for all of your friends!

Books, Books, Books!

On a sheet of paper, draw a picture of your favorite book. Write the title of your book on the paper. Then, finish this sentence and write it below your picture:

This is a good book to read because _____.

Rules to Read By

Make a sign of library rules. Write three rules on a piece of paper. Try to make your sign look fun and friendly. Hang your sign near your books.

Meet the Author and Illustrator

Angela Shelf Medearis

Lisa Campbell Ernst

Angela Shelf Medearis loves to read and go to the library. Lisa Campbell Ernst likes the library because it is a place that has surprises on every shelf. They both hope that you enjoy the library, too—just like Lucy!

For information about permission to reproduce selections from this book, write to trade.permissions@hmhco.com or to Permissions, Houghton Mifflin Harcourt Publishing Company, 3 Park Avenue, 19th Floor, New York, New York 10016.

www.hmhco.com

Green Light Readers is a trademark of Harcourt, Inc., registered in the United States of America and/or other jurisdictions.

Library of Congress Cataloging-in-Publication Data
Medearis, Angela Shelf, 1956–
Lucy's quiet book/Angela Shelf Medearis; illustrated by Lisa Campbell Ernst.
p. cm.
"Green Light Readers."
Summary: When the children's librarian gives Lucy a book to help her quiet her noisy brothers, Lucy learns the power of a story.
[1. Noise—Fiction. 2. Books and reading—Fiction. 3. Brothers and sisters—Fiction.]
I. Ernst, Lisa Campbell, ill. II. Title. III. Series: Green Light Reader.
PZ7.M51274Lu 2004
[E]—dc22 2003017483
ISBN 0-15-205144-9
ISBN 0-15-205143-0 pb

SCP 15 14 13
4500702357

Ages 5–7
Grades: 1–2
Guided Reading Level: F
Reading Recovery Level: 13

Green Light Readers
For the reader who's ready to GO!

"A must-have for any family with a beginning reader."—*Boston Sunday Herald*

"You can't go wrong with adding several copies of these terrific books to your beginning-to-read collection."—*School Library Journal*

"A winner for the beginner."—*Booklist*

Five Tips to Help Your Child Become a Great Reader

1. Get involved. Reading aloud to and with your child is just as important as encouraging your child to read independently.

2. Be curious. Ask questions about what your child is reading.

3. Make reading fun. Allow your child to pick books on subjects that interest her or him.

4. Words are everywhere—not just in books. Practice reading signs, packages, and cereal boxes with your child.

5. Set a good example. Make sure your child sees YOU reading.

Why Green Light Readers Is the Best Series for Your New Reader

● Created exclusively for beginning readers by some of the biggest and brightest names in children's books

● Reinforces the reading skills your child is learning in school

● Encourages children to read—and finish—books by themselves

● Offers extra enrichment through fun, age-appropriate activities unique to each story

● Incorporates characteristics of the Reading Recovery program used by educators

● Developed with Harcourt School Publishers and credentialed educational consultants